Go Away, Buddy!

by Karen Walberg • illustrated by John Speirs

Ana had a new brother.

Ana looked at her new brother.

"Can I hold my brother?" she said.

3

Ana held her new brother.

She liked him.

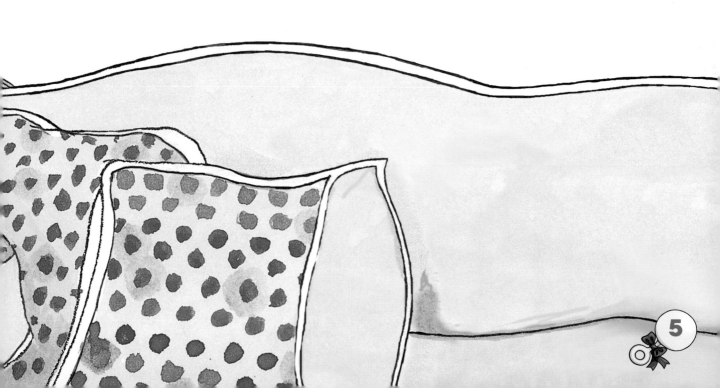

Buddy came over to look.

Ana said, "Go away, Buddy.

I am holding my new brother!"

Ana fed her brother.
She liked to feed him.

Buddy came over with his bowl.

"Go away, Buddy," said Ana.

"I am feeding my brother!"

Ana had the stroller.
She and her brother
were going for a walk.

Buddy came over with his leash.

Ana did not say, "Go away!"

Ana and the baby
went for a walk.
Buddy went, too!